P9-DXH-269

MEADOWLARK

MEADOWLARK

GREG RUTH · ETHAN HAWKE

A COMING-OF-AGE CRIME STORY

GRAND CENTRAL
PUBLISHING

NEW YORK BOSTON

Grand Central Publishing
Hachette Book Group
1290 Avenue of the Americas, New York, NY 10104
grandcentralpublishing.com
twitter.com/grandcentralpub

First Edition: July 2021

Grand Central Publishing is a division of Hachette Book Group, Inc. The Grand Central Publishing name and logo is a trademark of Hachette Book Group, Inc.

Library of Congress Control Number: 2020951333

ISBNs: 978-1-5387-1457-7 (hardcover); 978-1-5387-0592-6 (signed edition);
978-1-5387-0593-3 (special signed edition); 978-1-5387-1455-3 (ebook)

Printed in China

APS

10 9 8 7 6 5 4 3 2 1

Dedicated to our kids

- G&E

MEADOWLARK

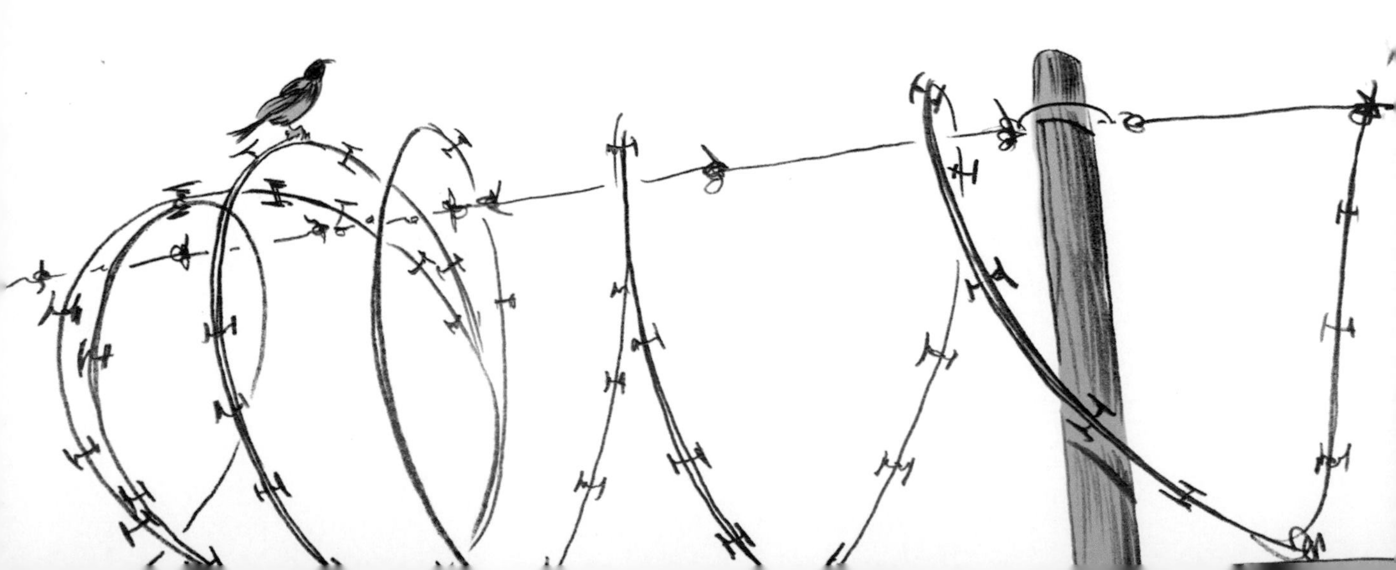

Fly, Coop!

But, Jack... he'll burn.
Nah.
He will be clothed in light.

The world **dies** over and over again...

...But the skeleton keeps walking.

Cooper!

Cooper!
Git yer ass out here now!

Honey...
...*What* happened to the *tires?*
Not just the *tires!*
That *danged* kid took the danged *wheels* off!
Jesus on *toast*, Loretta, I'm *already* runnin' *late* for *work!*
DOORS OPEN 8:00 PM
15 ROUNDS
NOV. 4
DEFENDING HIS CHAMPIONSHIP TITLE
JACK
JOHNSON
VS.
"RINGO" ROJAS

There you go, Dad.
Better.

I swear to God, Lo, that kid...
Cooper James Johnson, you get your butt out here right this minute!
Loretta, Cooper is out of control.
First the thing with school, and now...this!
They're not even close to being the same, Barry.
I can't believe you'd even
"...all day long I think of things, but nothing seems to satisfy..."
TEXAS
6 10

...He don't respect **you**, Sugar. And he **certainly** don't respect **me**.
You give that boy way too much **leash**.
If you're **shoppin'** for **respect**, Barry, driving around in another man's teenage **horn**-wagon **ain't** gonna get you there!
"Horn-wagon"?
Honey, **Excaliber** is an **original** fully restored 1978 Firebi
Jesus!
Children.
I am surrounded by children.

Where the heck you goin' now?
I'm calling Jack. He can come over and shovel this shitpile himself.
Then I'm gonna goddamned finish getting ready for work.
"Excalibur"? ...Really?
But...
...That's her name!

...But I do blame you, Jack!
I know exactly what kind of crap you put into his head.
Who was it that taught him to take a car apart like that?
Or that thing with the faucet?
Or hot-wiring Barry's old mower?
It sure as shit wasn't me!
No, it's not your damned car!
...Because until you pay the goddamned fifteen thousand dollars you owe us in child support...
...it's my fucking car, that's why!
Freeze right there, mister!
But...
...it's Dad. He's at the door.

I'm not wrong in hoping you just hid the rims some-place funny...
...rather than sold 'em on eBay or some shit.
Hey, Dad.
It's alright.
They're right there in the trunk.

You could hide a semi under Dinglebarry's nose and he'd never see it.
I know I'm supposed to be pissed at you...
...And I am...
...But it is a little bit funny.
Father of the year, Jack...
...Every year.
Hey there, Lo.
Look, I was just trying—
Can we take this inside?
You know... so as not to overplay our hillbilly mystique by having it out in front of the neighbors.
Yes, ma'am.

Hey, Jack
Barry.
So... I guess we missed the bus, huh?
You didn't tell him about school?
What's this about school?
Want me to call a cab?
We don't have time for this mess.
I got a better idea.

Jesus, Coop, you are...
...a calamity of epic proportions.
Okay, smart-ass. Grab your bag. Looks like I'm driving you to school...
...You can tell me all about whatever you did on the way.
Dad...
...I think Mom has other ideas...
Hey!

...Stole my goddamned car.
STOP

You can use our phone inside the—
I got my cell.
Jesus, Coop, where's your backpack?
Dad...
Hang on...
...Buck! Yeah, look...you gotta swing by Loretta's and pick us up.
Yeah... took off like Burt Reynolds just now.
Yes... again.

Yes...
...I know, Buck.
Don't sweat it.
Smokey owes me one anyway.

I know...
...Well, Buck, we ain't gonna be less late chatting on the phone all goddamned day!
We can wait inside if you want.
I found your old gloves, and—
Nah... Buck'll be here soon enough.
The hell is your bag for school?

You gotta stop calling him Dinglebarry,.
At least to his face.
Your mom loves him, Coop. Think about how that makes her feel, you runnin' him down all the time.

He shows up. Each day, every day. That's worth some basic respect.
Dad...Barry couldn't find his ass if it had a bell on it.
Good one.
Coop, I'm serious.
He squeaks when he and Mom are...going at it.
Squeaks.
He smells like old mayonnaise sitting in front of the TV every night in his tighty-whiteys.
Idiot-laughing at his game shows like some hairy SpongeBob.
That reminds me, Jack... You know that genius porn idea I had last week?
Buck. You see my kid sitting here next to us, right?
FORD

The one about that Trojan War, with the Cyclops penis...
...and the Hydra with them crop of titties?
Earl tole me the name of that movie? Ulysses? But we'll call it... Ulezzies!
Git it? U-lezzies?
I think we all get it, Buck.
Dad...
Okay, pard. No need to git yer panties in a—
Shit on a brick, Buck.
That was our turn!
2 mi

Three-point this heap and head on back to—
Dad, listen...
...about school.
Expelled?!
Expelled?!

FORD
How in the good goddamn did you get yourself expelled?
A joint... fell out of my bag in Mr. Pikett's class.
A joint.
Well, they also found an ounce in my locker...
...and a sheet or two of acid.

Pard...
...We really gotta shake a tail.
Yeah, Buck... hang on.
You.
Stay put.
SPEED LIMIT 70
65
FORD

Cooper.

Hello!
Earth to Cooper!

Goddammit, you better not be high right now.
I'm not!
Jesus!
FORD

Well, come on, then. You got your wish.
You're comin' with us.

"Take yer kid to work" day it *is*, then.

Two dead men at the North Gate!
Repeat: I spot two dead men at the front gate!
Second time didn't make it funnier, Leon!
Smokey said to find her in the Den when you got in, Jack.
HUNTSVILLE UNIT
OFFICIAL ENTRY ONLY

Park it
over by the
pumps...

At least you got Coop with you...
Smokes won't kill you outright with him around.
Let's not make the wish the father of the thought, Buck.
Well, I'm off to relieve Pete down at the SHU.
Remember your shift in the Tower.
Ain't forgot.
Listen to yer paw, kiddo.
Obey him in all things.
Alright, Buck.
See ya.
...Come on, then.

Remember what I told you, Coop...trees in a forest.

No eye contact with the wildlife.

Looky...
...Piggy has a piglet.
Red.
A month down in the SHU ain't helped your tan any.
We got lots to catch up on, Jackie boy.
Well, bless your heart, Red...
...You know my rule about talking with animals.
sniff
I got yer scent, Piglet.
I know... forests and trees.

Don't even, Jack...
...We're miles past what a knock might fix.
Loretta called and told me all about it...
She still worries after you, some.
Lo always had questionable tastes.
We're why Buck's late. Go easy on him. He's ready to piss himself.
Buck will never be too dumb to forget how smart you think you are, Jack.
Hey! Just look at ya!
Swear you git bigger each passing day!
Heya, Smokes.
How are you, Coop?
He's in deep shit, that's how he is.

Straight to the pokey, no trial, then, is it?
Unless the chair's back from the cleaners...
Can he hang with you while I do my rounds?
Now, what do you think?
You're also covering Pete's rounds. I volunteered you.
Alright, then.
What do we do when we're with Smokey, Coop?
"Obey her like she was God's own shotgun."
Close enough.

Hey, Smokey...
...How many of these guys, you know, get better? Get paroled or whatever?
Well, most of these boys aren't really the getting-better type.
They ain't all evil men...
...But they ain't here for doing good, either. Most are just screwups, some are broke inside, others... unfixably broken.
Since the cutbacks we been gettin' more 'n' more of the broken.

See that fella over there by the door? The goaty one all alone?
Did for his wife of twenty years with an old screwdriver.
Stabbed her over one hundred and thirty times.
...Jesus.
He was so far off his saddle it took ten troopers to subdue him,
He doesn't look like too big a deal.
That's because we fixed him.
Fixed him?
He was an undiagnosed paranoid schizophrenic. He just needed treatment.
Heavy doses of antipsychotics plus a constant flow of lithium...
...Fine as cream gravy now.

Part of me honestly wonders if leaving him crazy would be a mercy.
He ain't the man he was but he remembers everything that man did.
Every minute of every day.
So who did we lock up, then?
Who is it we think we are punishing?
The maniac criminal or the sweet, sad little man he hijacked?
That look like justice to you?
In the hall outside, Dad and I passed this freaky guy...
...Huge like King Kong or something. Albino white. Not so much bald as he was just taller than his hair. Gigantic.

Not the same kind of crazy, I'm sorry to report.
Not by miles.
Dad said something to him about...biting?
The bite... well, I think that's a story for your paw to tell you.
You always were six pounds of trouble in a five-pound bag.
Tell me anyway.
Okay, then.

"About a week or two back, we had this visiting nurse in from Houston running a yearly on Red, when he got ahold of her by the ponytail."
"She was about ninety pounds soaking wet, and Red was gonna snap her neck like a twig were it not for Jack rushing in and getting a chokehold on that boy right there on the floor of the infirmary."
"I have no doubt Red would've bit Jack's arm clean off had he not passed out first."
TIMED
WARDS
I thought chokeholds were illegal.
He told me he got that from a stray dog.
Coop, yer daddy's a hero to these men.
No one else had the stones to go into that room, 'cept for him alone...
...Ain't no one around here's gonna file a complaint but Red himself.

"And no one gives a shit what Red says."
Well...if it ain't Smokey's goon.
Stuck in first gear today, I see.
I'm catching up as we speak, Francis.
Gahdammit, I tole you...the name's Wolf Boy.
Lucifer
No matter how long you beg after it, ain't no one ever gonna call you that.
Especially while it says dumbass right there on your face.

Oh, for chrissakes.
...Idiots.

Like gazing into the **brain** of an **outhouse rat**, ***ain't*** it?
Jesus...
... You ain't ***kidding***, Smokes.
The ***crazy*** thing is, that's ***not*** even the ***craziest*** thing he's done this ***week***.
Bet you a ***cold*** Dr Pepp you ***can't*** finger the author of these ***horrors***.
You're ***on***.

Gotta be him.
Sorry...
Despite his prickly glare, Ace is actually about as sweet as a Sunday tea.
Holy cow... I think he went to my high school.
That he did. That there is Colton William Brady. Class of '02.
Colton was on the fast track to the NFL before he took a knife to his cheerleader girlfriend on prom night, under the bleachers.
When they found him...he was carving his crazy-ass poems into her open bones.

Wrong again.
Strike three, Coop.
Look up front...
...That beautiful white boy over there? Pretty as a pie supper?
No way.
Jesus, Smokey.
Beauty is a mask, Cooper...
...and behind this particular mask lies a hot bag of flies.

SOUTH TOWER/YARD
LOADNG GATE
Mornin', Jack.
Teddy.

Well, dang, Jack, sittin' here waitin' for you, I just about grew me a new beard...
...twice!
One of those days.
Sorry to leave you hangin', Pete.
Don't sweat it, kid. Yer just describing my every day.
That dang console behaving this morning?
So far, so good. But you know... give it a minute.

I hear Luby's got that three-berry pie in today.
Now, Smokey's punishing me with a double, so you go on now and get yourself a good long lunch.
Well, dang.
...I may just bring you back a wedge.
Well, thank you, Pete.
It's the Christian thing to do.

"Dad was good,
wasn't he?"

As a boxer, I mean.
Better than good, Coop. Ole Meadowlark was the real deal.
Took twenty punches to the face from some ape twice his rank in that exhibition bout in '92, and didn't stumble once before taking him down in the sixth.
A true marvel in the ring.
Got another? This one's all wrinkled.
Sorry, kid, at my age, it's all wrinkles.
Give it here.

If Dad was so great...why's he just a prison guard, then?
No offense.
Why's he get to have such high expectations for my life, but a low bar for himself?
Try not to misunderstand him, Coop...
...Your daddy don't see all, all the time.
We all want more for our children than our own reflections can afford, kid.
They say the hardest part about raising kids is when they're babies. Up all night, teething, and diapers...
Truth is, those are the easy times.
It's now, at your age, when it gets tricky. When you're old enough to make real and lasting mistakes.
You become a reflection of your parents' fears about themselves.

You asked me earlier about good and evil, and getting better.
All these convicts were somebody's baby once, just like my boy was...
...Just like you are your momma and daddy's baby now and always.
Pickin' through all that mess to discover your ownself ain't a kindness, Cooper...
...But it is a rare thing to find a truly evil person buried in the deep dark of it all.
That is not to say that the monsters don't exist.

Hey Smokey...
They can't... see us through this glass, can they?
Not really... it's fogged out from their side of things.
Why?

That's just the lockdown alarm!
Cooper, you need to head over to my office.
And lock yourself in.
Wait, what?
I'll have Hitler meet you there.
Uh... Hitler?
You'll get it when you see him.
Hustle up, kiddo.

Burt!
What in the ever-loving fuck is going on out there?
We're totally underwater down here!
Mick and ten stateys are on the way to you now!
Full-moon time down here, Smokey!
The Whiteys just jumped on the La Eme boys outta the fuckin' blue!
Brookes says we've got another fight breaking out in C-Block!
East End's gone quiet!
Jack!
What's going on at the South Tower?
Quiet here for now, Smokes...
...But the goddamned control panel just farted out on me!
Lights are green, but non-responsive!
Lockdown button...is dead too.

Red!
Snap out of it, man!
Eyes on the prize!
We're late already. Come on, now!

You two shit-tards ready?
They'll be comin' up behind us hard any minute.
Got our pig stickers nice 'n' sharp.
Just keep 'em busy as long as you can.
Don't forget to have fun.

Pretty Boy do his fuckin' part?
Yup.
Pulled the screws up last week just like he promised.
We should wait for him, right?
Lucifer
Fuck 'm.
We go. Now.
But Maurice said--
Hey fellas...
... The stabby guys out here wouldn't let me pass.
Jeezus, Colt, just get the fuckin' door.

Bill, y'all down at the Mess yet?
On our way now, Smokey!
Roger that.
Cooper... Jack's kid, right?

Yeah. You're um...
Used ta call me Big 'n' Tall, before the uh, conversation starter here.
Looky here.
Smokey tole me to keep you safe and you'd best believe that I surely will.
You scared, kiddo?
'Sides, I owe yer pappy, more 'n could ever be repaid.
Good man, that ole Meadowlark. You favor him some.
No.
A little bit, I guess. Yeah.

Don't be.
Either of my five boys would've pissed themselves twice for walkin' down these halls like you just now done.
Every so often the animals in the zoo just need to shake the cage a little.
Think of it like hurricane season in Corpus.
I'll be right outside, even so.
Ain't nothin' gonna happen way up here anyways.
If it does, well...
God hisself has yet to craft a prison shiv that can match a 12-gauge Remington in my thunderous paws.

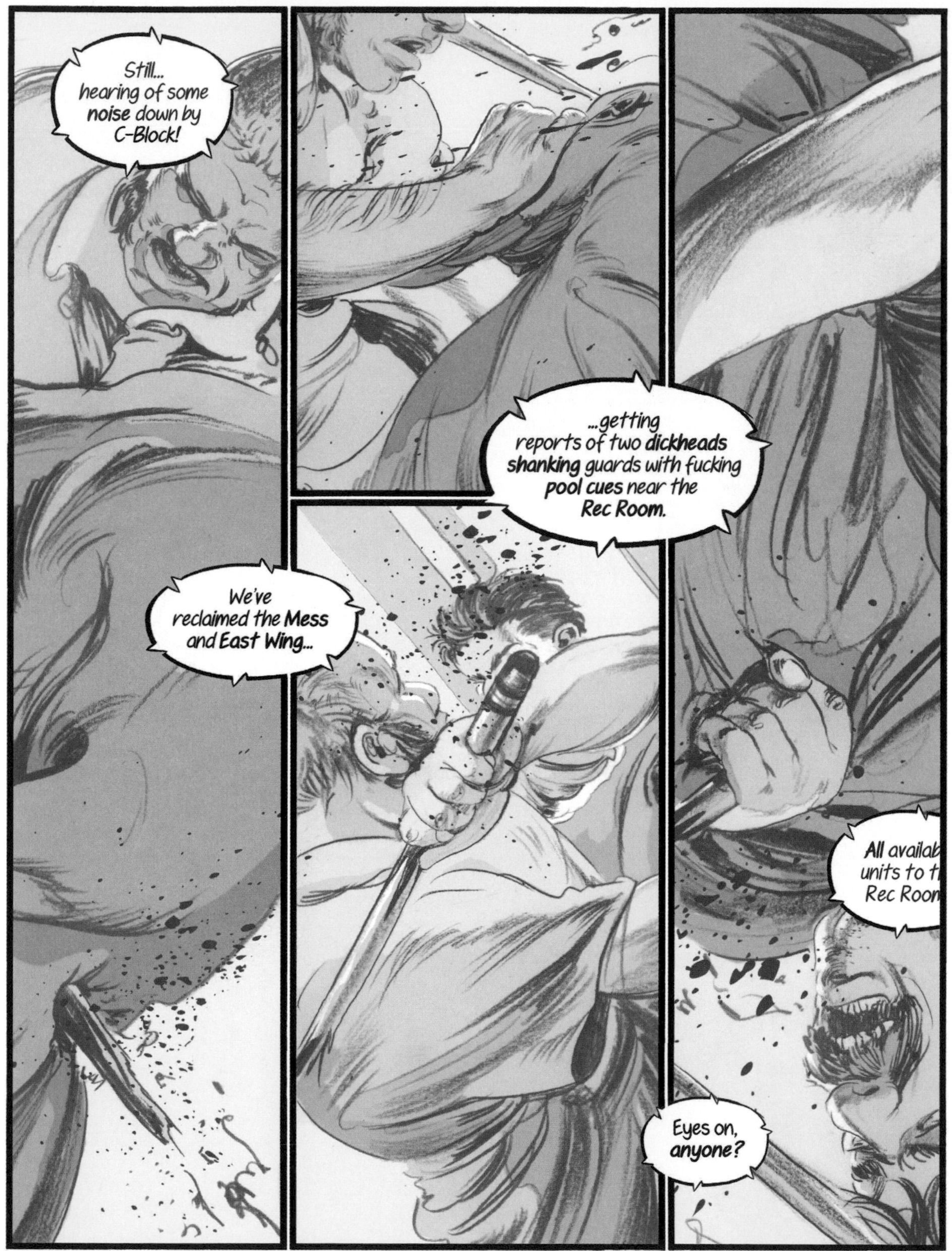

Still... hearing of some noise down by C-Block!
...getting reports of two dickheads shanking guards with fucking pool cues near the Rec Room.
We've reclaimed the Mess and East Wing...
All availab units to t Rec Room
Eyes on, anyone?

What the shit?
What?
Got three idiots running across the South Yard... with a sofa.
Did you just say a... sofa?
Damn.
I know what they're doing!

The outer gate's secure, right?
If I'm right, that won't matter!
Send anyone you can outside of the South Gate!
Right fucking now!
They're going over!

Luke, Pete... respond!
Roger that.
We have a decampment of three at the South Gate!
On our way, Smokey.
Code 552. Luke and Pete, report.
C-Block is locked down.
Jesus what
mess.
Local and state troopers heading in.
Do we have an ETA on medics?
I've got three down he in B-Block!
We have a bad door here.
I'm seeing reporters
north
Roger.
On our way!
Mess is locked
Jesus...
Jack, report backup when they've arrived.
We need aramedics down here, now!
Who's got a report on the Mess Hall for me?
I found Pete.
I need
R.T. and anyone
the area to
South Gate
now!
We need a hand down in B-Block!
Repeat... I've found Pete.

"So, here's what we know so far."
"It started in D-Block. Then North Hall and the Mess all exploded into burly brawls, and once there was blood in the water, the whole place lit up like a Christmas tree..."
"...But this wasn't just some spiced-up riot, this was all meant to ink the waters as cover for the breakout."
"Colton Brady, Red, and Wolf Boy used that Rec Room couch to ladder over the South Gate as you saw...but someone on the inside had to have helped them make sure it was loose for their run."
"Only a guard would've had access to the tool to lift those bolts."

"Guess Pete had come back early to gift you with a slice of three-berry pie."

"His killers are both currently high-fiving it in the SHU until I can find God's forgiveness for this shit storm."

...Pete.
I got **dead officers**, six **more** in the infirmary nursing **stab** wounds, least a **dozen** inmates in varying states of **broken**.
Local **and** national press are out there right now to tear me **six** new holes if I don't un-ring this bell by **yesterday**.
It's an absolute **nightmare**, Jack.
Any **idea** how this happened yet?
...
No one's seen **Buck** since the **can** opened up, Jack.
Any idea where he might be now?

No...
Not since... he dropped me and Coop off this morning.
You don't think that he—
Right now, Jack, you're the only one I'm not worried about.
The hell happened with the lockdown gates?
Whole system was ancient when LBJ was in office, Smokes.
You could bring it down with a sneeze.
Bad enough to have Red on the loose...
...but Wolf Boy and Colton? Where the hell did that courtship come from?
Don't think I ever seen 'em even look at each other before today.

I think it's time we get you clear of all this mess, Cooper.
Alright, Dad.
Sorry for all the ruckus, kiddo.
Next time we'll do something less...horrible.
Like...go to the dentist, maybe.
Heh.
We'll head around back to avoid the crowds.
But... we'll need a ride.
I heard...
...ain't never been a car so shitty that's been stolen so often.
Chet can drive you out.
Come straight back for the debrief, okay?
Roger that, Smokey.

Okay.
We're just about clear of 'em, gentlemen.
Where we headed to, Jack?

We need to get my car at Huntsville Memorial.
So that's where she took it.

Turn here.

Up over there.
Loretta never did abide a parking garage. Even in broad daylight.
Dad?

Don't bring me back to Mom.
Take me with you.
I want to come live with you.
You know... like we talked about.
I told you, I gotta go back to the prison and deal with this mess.
She's waiting for you inside.
Mom is mad at me all the time...
...If I have to hear Barry call me "chummo" one more time, I will seriously lose my mind, Dad.
Jesus Christ, Coop, this?
Now?
Goddammit.

...Get out.
I don't have time for any more damn games.

Oh, you're smiling right now?

This is all so damn fun for you?
Ritchie's wife is gonna put three fatherless girls to sleep tonight,
but fuck 'em.
You got yours, right?

Pete's wife's gonna face that cancer alone now.
A man I've known since I was your age died today, do you get that?
When did it all become about you anyway?
I don't walk this earth to buy you shit or take you to the movies!
You think I don't still have hopes?
You think you're the only person in town with fuckin' dreams?
Christ almighty!
Don't start that shit!

Why are you yelling at me like this?
Because you always fucking do this!
You start crying whenever I start telling you the truth!
...And then I'm supposed to shut up and feel like an asshole!
So...thanks again for that particular brand of bullshit.

Dad...
What are we doing here?
MOTEL

MOTEL OFFICE
There's something I gotta take care of before we head back.
Just sit tight. I won't be long.
What, you got a girlfriend here or something?

Jesus fucking Christ!
Can I not rely upon you to do one fucking thing I ask?

...Sorry.
Coop...
...I know things feel a little...out of control.
Believe me, they are off the fucking turn for me too.
I just...
...I love you, buddy.
...Whatever, weirdo.

sKRrrt...
...sKRrrt...
a cold steel
rail...
...a sm-
sKRrrt...a
veil...

...Hot ashes for trees...
...sKRrrt...
...sKRrt Did you exchange...
...a walk-on sKRrrt...
...sKRrrRt lead role in a cage...

...sKRrrt
...skrrRt...
...sKRrrt
lost souls
sKRrrt...skrt
fishbowl...
...skrRtt...
sKRrrt...

...sKRrrt... old fears...
...sKRrrTt...
Well, Jack, there ain't no fuckin' sunshine for you or any of us...
...Not until those cartel fucks get their pound of flesh.

Goddamn Jack...
... You brought your fucking kid?

What the shit?
Coop?

Let me get that for you, son.
I know this is Texas, Jack...
...But is this really the best toy choice for your son?
Maurice... look, I didn't know...
Boy's got yer eyes, Jackie...
Coop.
Go back and wait in the car like I asked you to.
No.
The boy stays.

Maurice, Cooper doesn't know anything about anything.
Well, dang, Jack, thanks to you he sure as hell does now.
Don't he?
Colt.
Make room for the kid over by Red and Wolfie so we can finish our chat.
Like a girls' bathroom at a school dance up in here.
Sure thing, bossman.
Pull up a chair, Jack.
Let's get everything out in the open, shall we?

Maurice...
...What the hell is happening here?
It's you, Jack, that disappoints me the most.
Don't you know by now? The mouse does not toy with the cat.
Where's Buck?
Lucifer
But we can play it your way if you like...
...You lie to me about where the money's at, and I'll pretend I don't already know.

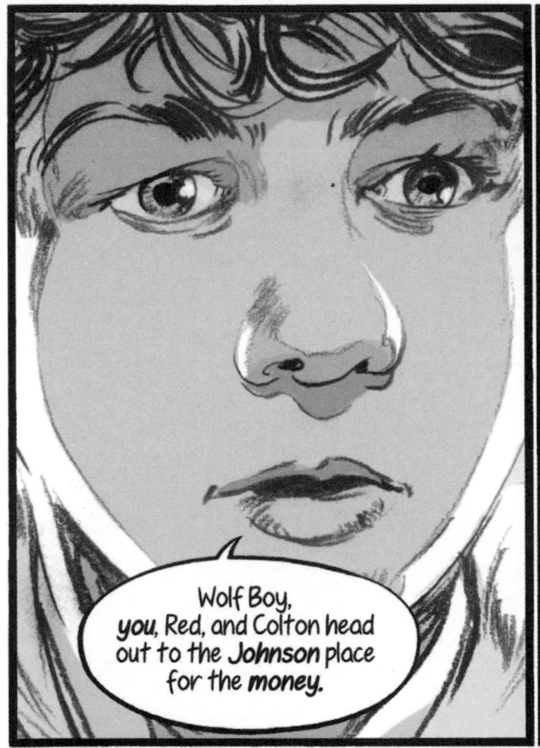
Wolf Boy, you, Red, and Colton head out to the Johnson place for the money.

It's under the bed in Cooper's room... behind the Rock 'Em Sock 'Em Robots.

Take the El Camino out back.
Jack's gonna need Buck's truck for the drive to Juarez after.
I don't trust his shit-wagon to make it to the fuckin' mall.

Uh...
...Not sure Red can fit in the El Camino, Maurice.
Lucifer
It's a car that's a pickup.
Figure it out.

Well... Jack, **where** to **begin**, eh?

I need to use the **restroom.**

Son, you know what **me** and **owls** got in **common?**

We **each** don't give a **hoot.**

To your **left.** Handle **sticks** a little.

Buck?
Jeez, Buck...what are you—

"You know what disappoints me the most, Jack?"

It's the disloyalty.
After all our years together. This betrayal...
...Makes my skin hot, just thinking about it.
You know?
Like I got my period or some shit.
Maurice, look...
Cooper is just a kid. You can't—
I thought you plumb fell in.
Well, dang, son!

...Coop?
He looks scared, Jack.
Yer daddy and I are getting to the good part.
Grab a seat right yonder, Cooper.
Ole Jack here ever tell you about his big fight with Ringo?
Back in... '83, wasn't it?
Dad?
Not now, Coop.

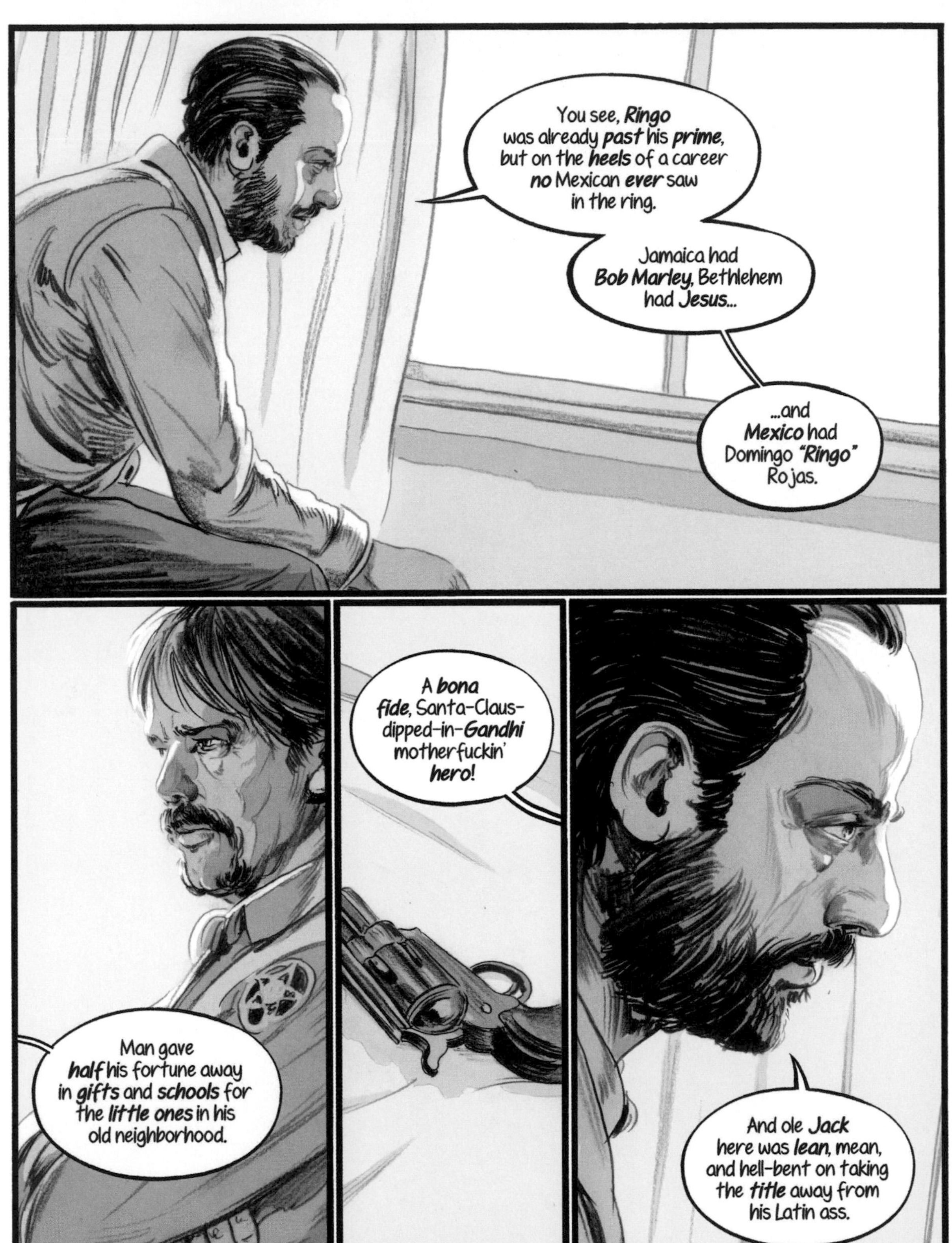
You see, Ringo was already past his prime, but on the heels of a career no Mexican ever saw in the ring.
Jamaica had Bob Marley, Bethlehem had Jesus...
...and Mexico had Domingo "Ringo" Rojas.
Man gave half his fortune away in gifts and schools for the little ones in his old neighborhood.
A bona fide, Santa-Claus-dipped-in-Gandhi motherfuckin' hero!
And ole Jack here was lean, mean, and hell-bent on taking the title away from his Latin ass.

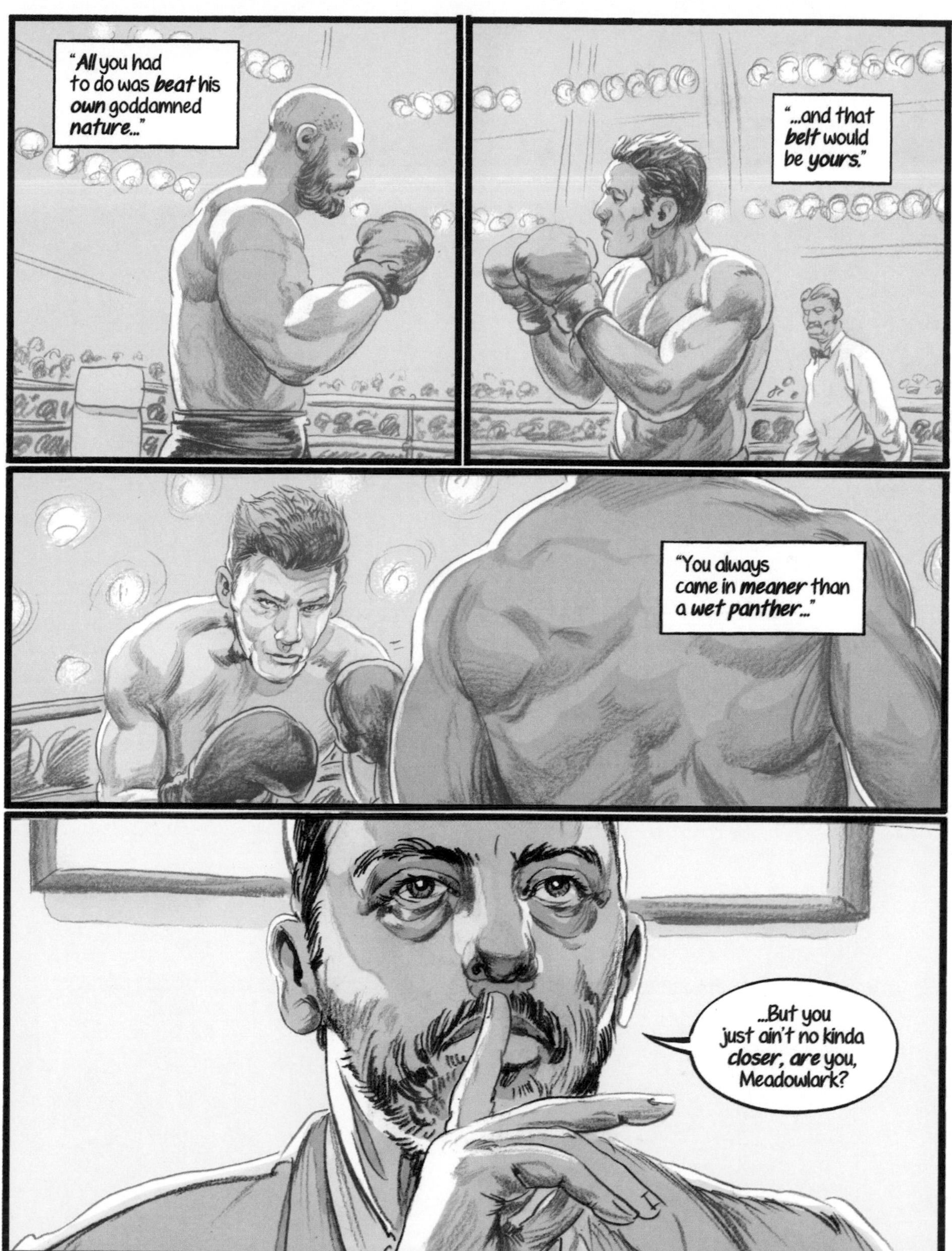
"All you had to do was beat his own goddamned nature..."
"...and that belt would be yours."
"You always came in meaner than a wet panther..."
...But you just ain't no kinda closer, are you, Meadowlark?

Yer daddy, Coop, is the special kind of loser who can struggle the car right up to the intersection...
...and just plumb stalls out when the light goes green.
That's how you let Ringo beat you silly that night in Houston.
And all the Ringos that came before and after.
It's just more tits on a bull, Maurice.
And this tough-guy spooky gangster horseshit?
You think I don't know what you're trying to do here?
I'm just a weather vane, Jack.

I don't make the wind blow.
Your kid is gonna watch you die first.

Ah!

Nng...

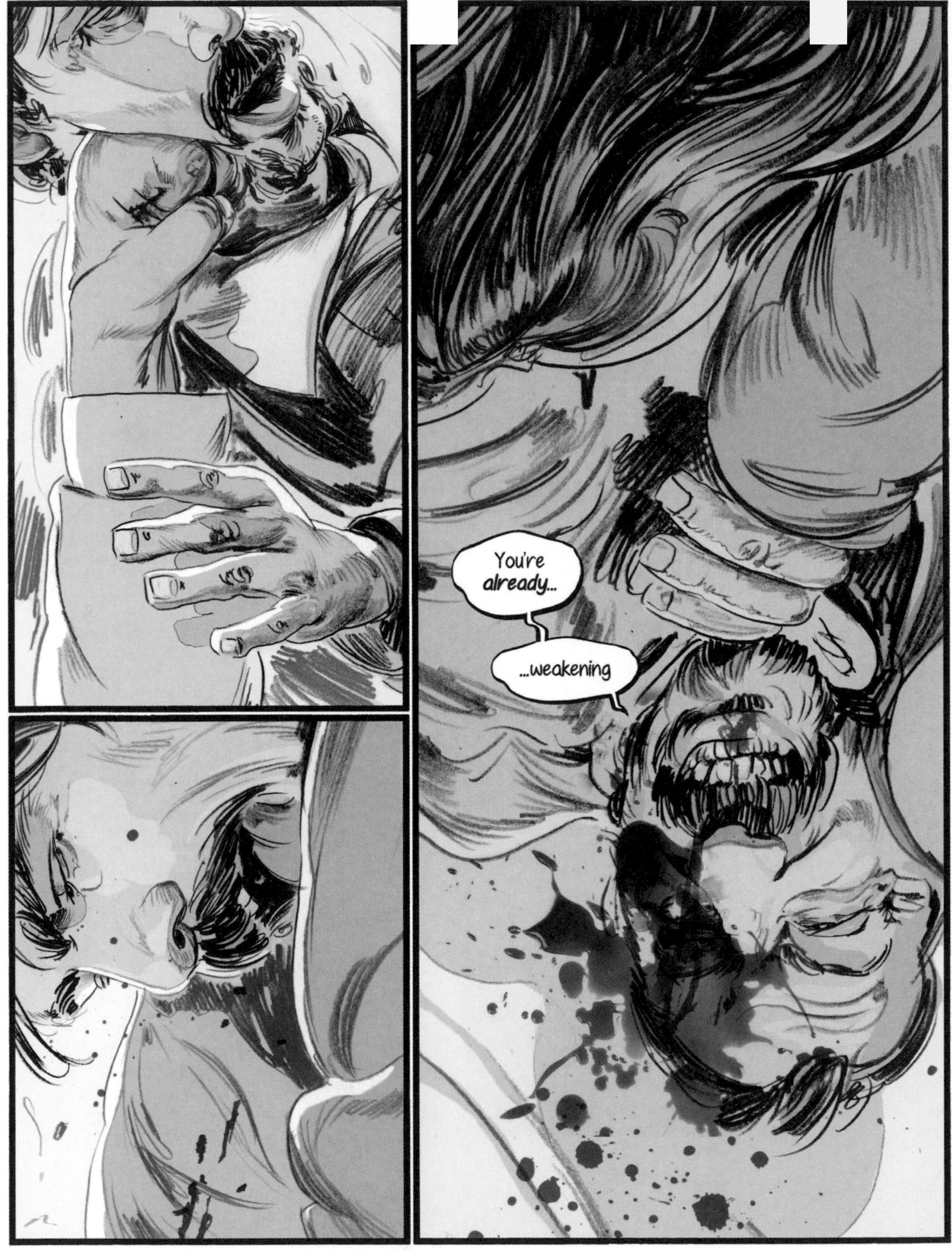
You're already...
...weakening

Urk!

Nngg..
Ah!

Dad!
Poor...
...Jack.
Still...
can't close...
You
know what,
Maurice?
Fuck
you!

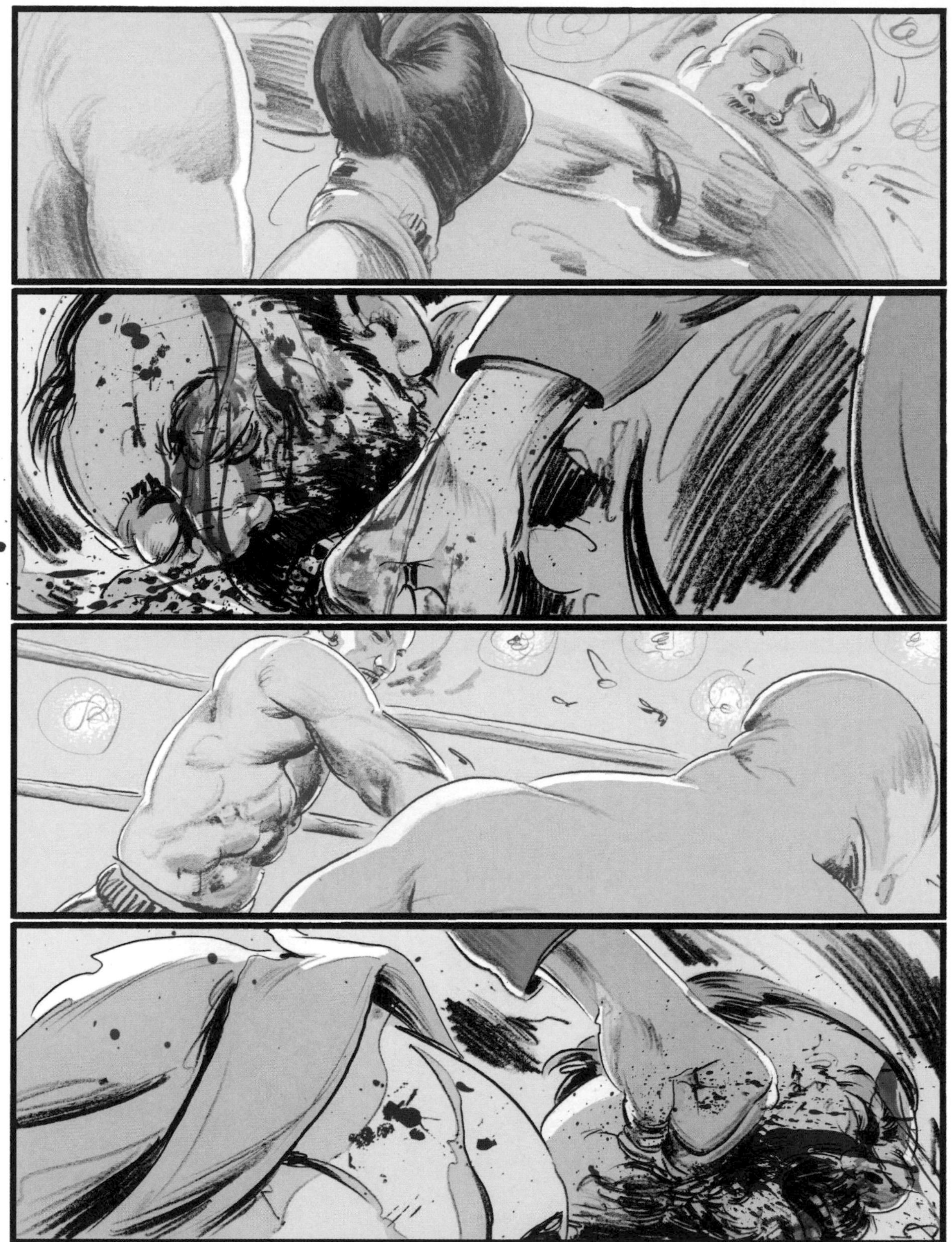

Oh my God.

Dad?
I'm alright, Coop.
It's okay.
But your leg...
Leave it.
Right now it's the only thing keeping me from bleeding out.

How are you?
Are you hurt?
No— I'm okay.
Buck's... dead.
Yeah.
I know.
We should...
What are we going to do?
We have to get after them.
Do you have my keys?

Get after them?
Are you kidding me?
You can barely stand up! We have to get you to a hospital!
No...time for that.
Shit...
Only four rounds left,
Why do they think there's money at the house?
Buck...must have said something about it.
It's complicated.

What the **hell**, Dad?
Complicated? You just ***killed*** a man!
Stay here.
Call the ***cops*** and tell them what ***happened***. I have to ***go*** and stop these animals.

What the ***fuck***, Dad?
Can you even ***hear*** yourself?

Who do you think you ***are***? The ***sheriff*** of fucking ***Dodge City***?

I am one epic, galaxy-class fuckup, Coop!
Haven't you picked up on that by now?
Jesus! Look at your father!
Do I strike you as someone with a fucking plan here?
I'm also an idiot for putting you in this much danger already!
You need to stay here.
No way. I'm coming with you.
Come on, then.
You can be mad at me on the way.

Dad...
...You sure you're okay to drive?

Dad...
your leg's really
bleeding.
A lot.

Might have
something to do with
the knife jammed
up inside it.

Dad...I'm serious.
I know. Look, you weren't supposed to be here today.
I wanted to keep you away from all this until it was done.
I'm just trying to keep you safe.
You call this safe?
Fair point.
How do you even know these scary people?
Maurice used to manage me back in my boxing days.

See...
...Buck and I got into some... *trouble* with Maurice...
...Springing those *animals* and *stashing* his *traveling* money was how we *squared* it.
Buck wasn't ever supposed to *be* at the damn *motel.*
POLICE
0824

Hello?

Sorry, what?
Did you hear anything I just said?
You look... funny.
Huh?
I said your eyes look weird.

...late
for **school**...

Dad!

What?
Me...driving right now...with this thing in my leg...
...You gotta...take the wheel, Coop.

SPEED LIMIT 85
Like puttin' socks...on a rooster.
Help me with my belt.
Gotta tourniquet this motherpisser.
But... Dad, I can't drive.

Ngh...
One of many in my catalog of failures as a father to ya, Coop.
Hop up front and we'll figure it out.
It's easier than you think.
Not too much different than them video games you made me play last Christmas.
I really think it is.
Turn the key, push the gas to get 'er goin'.
Uhmm... Okay, gimme a sec...

There you go.
Now, foot on the brake...put it into drive, and let's—
WhOah!
Brakes, brakes!
Okay, it's okay.
Deep breath and try again.
Jesus, Dad! I can't do this!

But your mom and Barry are gonna come home to find those three killers lookin' for money they won't find.

Ain't no cop or nurse gonna save them from what they'll do to them in time except us.

I won't ever ask you to do something like this again...
...but we have to go.
Now.
Okay.
Alrighty, then.
Foot on the brake, put it in drive... and very slowly, press on the gas.

Great. You're a total natural, Coop.
Be quick but don't hurry.
Take Brazos over to the I-30. We can cut through the east side and buy some time.

You are goddamned whip-smart and capable of anything...
...You know that, right?
I know I don't say it enough...
...but you've got nothing but choices and opportunities ahead of you...

At my age... it's all just juggling consequences.
A chance to get out from under the weight of that came along, and I went for it.
I was stupid.
Fucked it all up like I do most things.
I just wanted to get out of my crappy apartment and set us up in a nice place together.
I wanted your college paid for and a stake for yourself after...
Take a right here down this alley.

Maybe I also wanted to stick it to him at the same time.
...And Maurice was a lot of things but none of them good.
Guess I just wanted a way out for you from this grubby life.
A place for you to be happy.
I was happy, Dad!
I love that crappy apartment. Sleeping on your sofa in front of the TV and getting Egg McMuffins for breakfast.
Leaving the dishes too long in the sink.

It was my life and it didn't need to be better.
I was happy even if I didn't show it enough.
And what have we got now, huh?
Look at what we're doing!
Explain to me how all this is a fucking improvement.

Well...just because you got ideas don't mean you have a plan.
Fair point.
What is that?
Stop the car.
Stop!

I think we **found** 'em.

Stay **here** while I check this out.

This **can't** be like at the **motel**. You need to **listen** to me this time.

...Okay

I'm serious as a heart attack about this, Coop.
Got it. I'll be right here.
I won't go anywhere. Promise.
I won't go far...
Shout or honk the horn if you see anything funny.

Damn.
What?
They have a gun now.
They're probably still around.
Let's go.

I think we should go now.
Don't you?
Too late!
Rowrf! Aroof!

Urf!
Coop?
Oh no.
Eat yer fuckin eyes out!

Get off!
Get off!

Cooper!
Are you hurt?
Where's he at?
Just burst through the window...
...Howling like a dog or...
I don't... know.
What the hell is he, Dad?
Not an actual wolf, thankfully for the rest of us.
You sure you're not hurt? That was some crash.

Guess I flunked my driving test, Coach.
You kiddin' me?
That was some Steve McQueen ninja-fighting mojo you just—
What?
RDNK-1
Just some dumb ole 'dillo.

Cooper...
...Very casually come up and out of the car and follow me now.

Just act like we're fine and safe and alone.

Good news is, if Francis had that cop's gun he'd have used it by now.
I need you to hang out in the middle of the road, while I check the woods back over there.
Stay low and perk yer ears.
You hear anything, stay down.
I'll be close.
Dad!
Dad?

Where's yer daddy at, boy?

Kef... what the fuck, Jack?!
I was just...kef...playin', goddammit.
You alright, Coop?
...Yeah.
Ain't no alrights no more!
Kef.
Ain't none of you gonna be alright when you tell Maurice whut you done to his Wolf Boy!
Tell him yourself, Francis.

Sorry for that, Coop.
Couldn't see any other way to it. There's going to be blood. We're gonna have to fight.
I know. It's okay.
It's not, though. None of this is, and I want you to know I see it.
I think you killed my car.
Though...many people would call it a mercy.

Red and Colton left their wheels here.
See? Those tracks lead off into the woods...
...Blood too.
Kyle and I would sneak out here to blow up logs with M-80s when we were kids.
I know a shortcut to the house.
We can still beat 'em there.

Jesus, Dad...
You can't do this. Your leg...
I don't want to hear that kinda shit from you anymore!
But, Dad, please...

We cannot talk, worry, or fucking doubt our way out of this particular shit storm, Cooper.
Please tell me you fucking get this.
Sorry.
Didn't mean to holler at you like that.

No...it's *okay.*
Sometimes I think the reason *why* I don't make *sense* to *you...*
...is because you're not old enough to have *failed* at anything yet.

You cannot yet imagine what it's like...
...seeing your dreams glare back at you from the mirror every day you put on your prison guard uniform.
You ask why I don't like to come around the house.
It ain't you or your mom or even Barry.
It's that dang room of yours, Coop.
Cuts me right open every time I go in there.
Those old boxing gloves you keep and that poster you've hung over that old air vent...
...Like a goddamned shrine to everything I'm not but what you wish I was.

I can't figure out how I'm supposed to live up to that...perfect image you have of me...
...And that has, on many an occasion, turned me asshole, and I am sorry for it.
I never needed you to be perfect, Dad.
I just needed you to be around.

Given our current situation, I'd file that under being careful what you wish for.

We cut through that stand of *trees*, we'll *be* there.
Yeah... I *see* now.
Good. That's good.

I ain't a hunter myself...
...but way I heard tell it, the idea is to foster silence.
You chatty Cathys are more fun than soap opera night on C-Block.
Whoa, pard. Hang on, now.
Where's Red got to, Colton?
Heh.
Better luck pickin' up a turd by the clean end than unraveling Red's mystery.
It's just us chickens.

Guess this means ole Wolf Boy's gone to Jesus.
Yer lookin' a little peaky yerself...
Put it down, Colton.
The truth is never quite what you expect...
...Is it, Meadowlark?
Shuffling along when you thought you'd be struttin'...
...Falling when flying was called for.
Alright, Colton...
...You bag-of-cats crazy motherfucker...
...I'll give you what you're after. So let's both drop our guns and step to it.
Count of three... good?
Good don't come close.

One...
Two...
Three.

Ow!
That smarts!
Cheater!

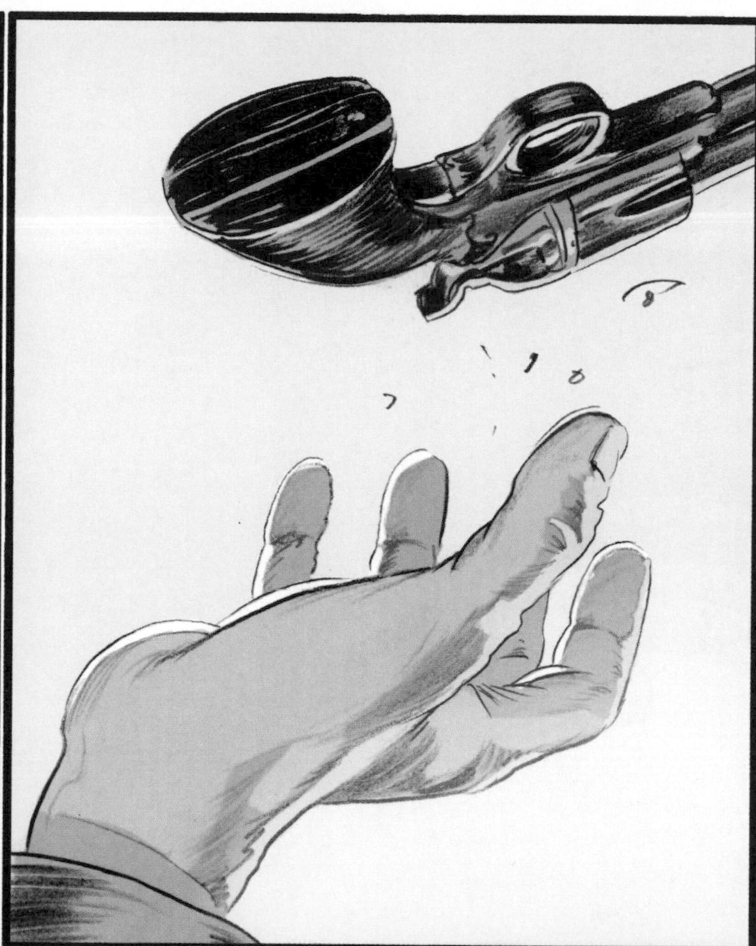

Dad!

Fuck almighty!
That is some unsportsmanlike shit right there, Meadowlark.
Now I s'pose I'll just haveto shoot you in front of your damn kid.
...Back, Coop.
Aw... who am I kiddin'?

...This ain't worked since Red beat that hillbilly cop to death with it.
See? Brains.
So.
Now that we're both pretty as pie suppers...
Let's try this ag—
Urk!

Do you not ever know when to...
...shut...
...the fuck..
...up!?

Stay down, Colton.
It don't have to end here.
kaf!
...There's... somethin' on yer leg.
Oof!

Whoop!
Whoop!
Hang on...
...Missed a spot.
Stop!

I said stop, goddammit.
Cooper...
...no.
Hurk!

Dad!
gUrk..
Use...yer dick-bone...
...As a straw...for my Vanilla Coke.
Epic... last words... Colt.

Jesus, Dad...your leg.
Why'd you do that? I had your gun!
No...
...You'll need that last bullet for what's next.
Aw... you're bleeding everywhere...
We have to get you over to a hospital before—
Ain't...no stopping that now, son.
...Need to tell you about... poster in your room...Red...

You know what...taught me the most about fighting?
"Not my old trainer at the gym...or all those fights that followed on after."
...kaf
"When I was about your age, mostly to get my ass outta the house and away from your grandma..."
"...I worked a long summer at the Houston Zoo."
ZOO
ENTRANCE

"Hotter than hell's pepper patch, and the stink of every animal's butthole in creation made my eyes water every morning I came in to work."
"Pay was worse."
"I loved it."
Dad...
No... important...
...Listen

"I fed 'em... the animals."
"Little ones at first. Snakes, beavers... you know."
"But soon...I was tossing grub to the big cats."
Weren't like the movies...
...Throwing raw steaks to giant maws or shit like that.

"Mostly it was like feeding...a dog."
"Pouring kibble into a trough."
"Even so, perched behind sleepy prisoner's eyes that old animal self was there..."
"...crouched and watching for its moment. That spark of violence was always there."
"Watching you, hoping you might be the one to bring it to him."
Animals ain't got no sense of time.
Kef!
No tomorrow, no yesterday.
When they do a thing it's all they do.

People hold back when they fight...try to protect.
Worry over what losing a tooth might look like....
That kind of thinking in a fight with an animal is losing.
"Worry is thinking, on a bent knee, Cooper. Animals don't play that game."
"Dad...I don't understand."
That's how Red will come at you.
That's how he kills you.

Don't let him.
...Okay.
You know, Coop...

...I never regretted losing a fight...
...Only regret...
...when I stopped fighting.

Good night,
Dad.

Shit.
Shit, shit.
Shit.

What do
I do.. what do
I do?

911

9-1-1. What's your
emergency?
Hi, uh...
I need to report
a...burglary.
It's, um,
one of the guys...
convicts who escaped
the prison today.

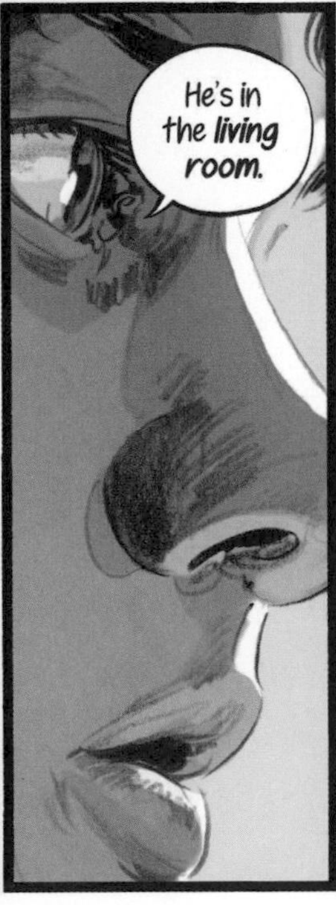
He's in
the living
room.

Ma'am,
what's your
location?
I'm not a
ma'am.
My name's...
Cooper.

Excuse me?
Cooper Johnson. That's my name.
My father is...was Jack Johnson. He worked at the prison.
He's... dead.
They...killed him. In the woods.
That... football player. The crazy one...I forget his name.
Colton... something.
He's dead too.
Are you aware it's a crime to prank call emergency services?
This isn't a goddamned prank call!
I need help! Right now!
I can't do this! I'm...supposed to but...I can't!
Ma'am, I need you to calm down.
Goddammit!

Ow!
Hurm?

...Smell you, Little Pig...

Guess ole' Maurice dint have the stones to do a kid...
Jesus...

snif.
... But since yer flying solo tonight, guess he sent yer Paw to the other side of the grass.

That's too bad...

... I wanted to do it.

Way I see it, this goes one of two ways.
I could tear the head off yer body and leave it lying here for yer momma to come home to...
Or...
...You can just spill where yer daddy's money's hid, and I'll be on my way.

...Maybe I get
creative with
her after.
Don't *hear* no
Barney Fifes comin' to
yer *rescue*, Piglet.

So it's just the two of—
clik

Eh?
Oof!

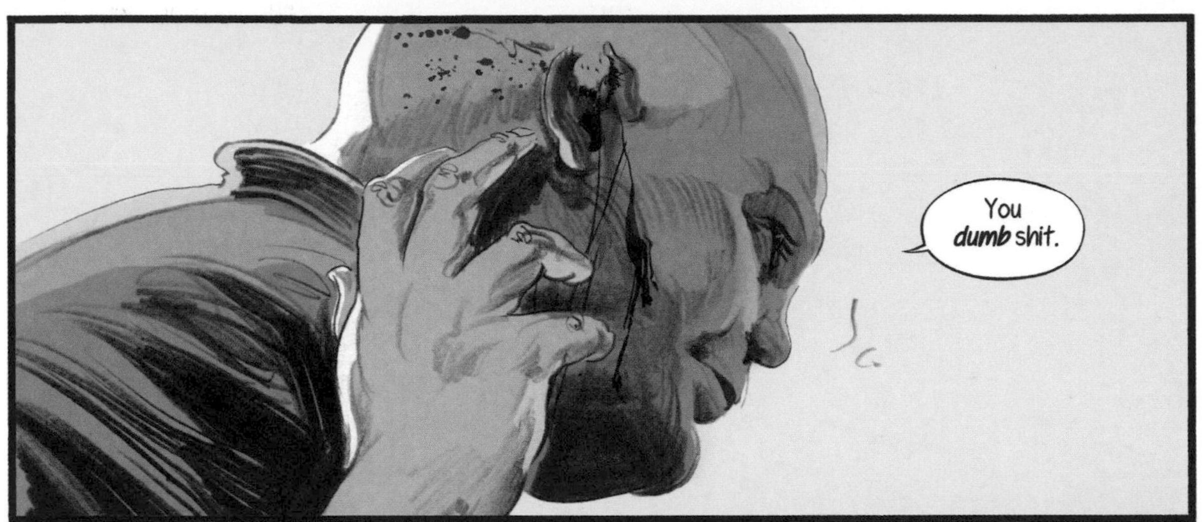
You *dumb* shit.

You *watch* too many *movies*.
nNghh...

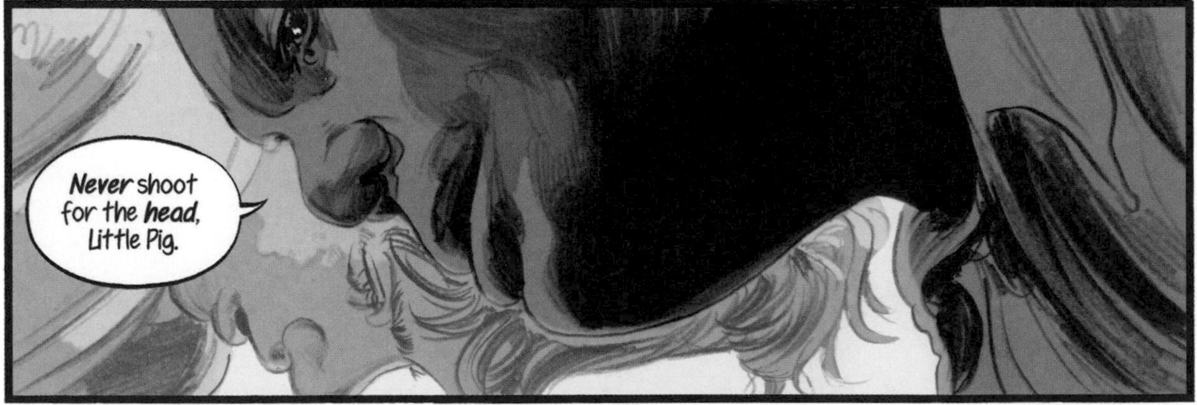
Never shoot for the *head*, Little Pig.

wurk

Where is it?
W-what?
The money.

I don't know anything, I swear.
I don't believe you.

nNgh...
Better if you know, Piggy.
Better if you tell.
Otherwise...
...you got no use.

So...tell me a story, Little Pig.
Ow.
Heh...now, where do you think you're going?

Gotcha!
Ah!

A pig in a tree...
...waiting for me...
I don't know.
I don't know about anything.
Liar!

GraAh!

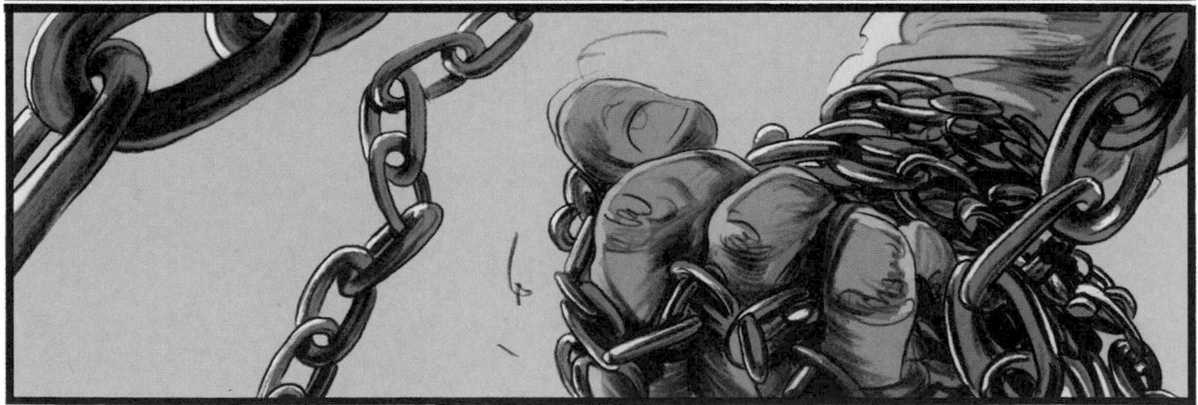

GAK!

hUrk!
AarRr!!
nNGh...
GLurr...

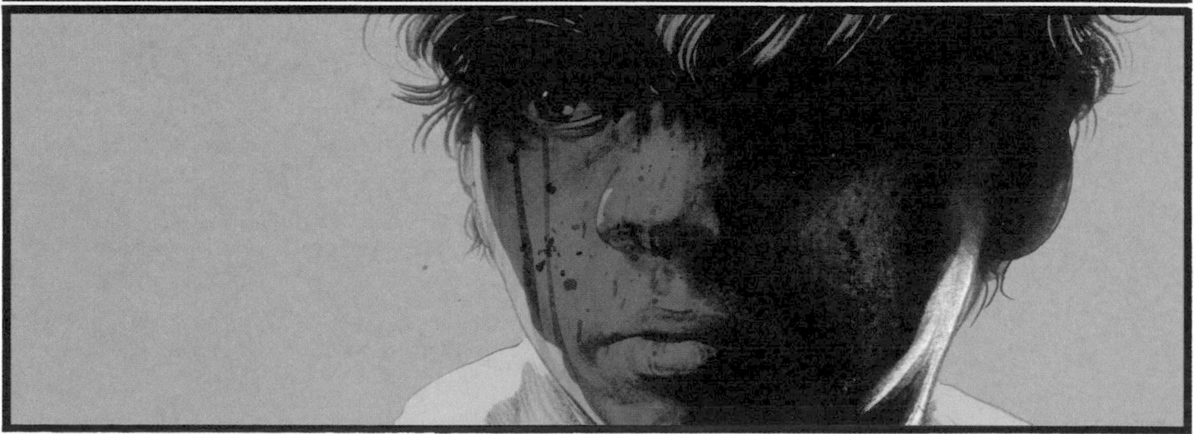

TWO WEEKS LATER

Cooper!

Cooper, I'm leaving for work!

Cooper!
I'll be out front. Coffee's in the pot.
Kitchen's still a mess, so... wear shoes!
Okay, Mom!
On my way!

ADMISSION $5.00
DOORS OPEN 8:00 PM
ONE NIGHT ONLY!
15 ROUNDS
NOV. 4
CHAMPIONSHIP TITLE
PINK FLOYD
Hey, Dad...
...Today's the day.

"...May have been instrumental in the very prison break they were supposed to be stopping."
"KBTX's own Rugg Tuggler asked Warden Maria "Smokey" Cortez about this shocking new development."

"All I can comment on right now is that a brave young boy..."
"...lost his father while stopping these criminals."
"I will not hang a man in public for protecting his son, his family, and this community on your every rumor."

"However...I do promise you all that the full and factual truth will come out on this tragedy."
"We all want the same thing, and you know me well enough to know I won't stop in this investigation."

"You should expect no less than that."

"But...if you think I'm the sorta gal who'd chum yer feeding frenzy with a grieving boy's dead daddy, well..."
"...then we ain't met, and I don't have time for strangers right now."
"Next question."
Hey, Mom...
...wasn't Barry driving you in today?
He is. Got up early to pick his new company car...
Greased lightning, he is not.
True.
Found yerself some breakfast I hope?
Yeah...I got coffee.

At least get you some real food after I leave?
There's still tons of leftovers from the service.
'Fraid Barry found where I'd hid the ribs...
...He missed the hush puppies, though.
Okay. Maybe later.
What you said at the funeral...
...It was beautiful, Cooper.
Your daddy would have been so proud.
I really miss him.
Me too, kiddo.

What they're saying on the news about your father...
It's alright.
I don't care.
Really.
Hey!
Hands off my woman, buster!
Ew, Barry...
Pretty bitchin' wheels, Barry.
Right? Even got that Bluetooth!
McCURRY INSURANCE
Hey, Coop... Maybe after work we'll take ole Excalibur out for a spin?
Break in that new license.
Sure.

Hey, Mom,
By the time you read this...I'll be gone.
I'm not sure where I'm heading to yet, but I promise to let you know as soon as I get there.
I don't want you to think my leaving is about you or Barry.
I'm not running away from either of you.
I just need to go.

I'm sorry for how I've been these last couple years, and for what we brought home to you both.
I know Dad was.
... And I figured we both wouldn't let me go if I tried to say goodbye in person.
Under my bed, you'll find a little over five hundred thousand dollars in cash.
-mom
dc
It's from the money that cost Dad his life. He'd want you to have it too. Pay off the house, get a decent car...
...Build the kind of life with Barry you've been wanting.

Tell Barry I'm sorry about taking the Firebird, but it's the only thing I had left from Dad that he was proud of.

I don't want you to worry about me. I'm okay... (I didn't leave you all of the money).

I'm not running away from anything here. It's important to me that you understand that.

I'm running toward something.

...And I'm going
to go meet it.

I'll see you again.
Love you,
—Cooper

And so off he went,
as well as he could,
over the roil and waves of the land.

Even as the storms of the day rose and crashed,
the houses and trees
blown down as the mountains trembled,
he went.

The black sky, thunder-clapping its lightning on the sea
that crowned with foam clutching after him,
The young man cried out without being able to hear his own words,
aimed his heart
towards the bright breach in the darkling sky,

and chased it.

—From "The Fisherman and His Wife"
Collected by the Brothers Grimm, 1812

I'd like to thank my wife, Jen, and my two boys, Nate and Emmett, for their endless inspiration and support. Thanks also to Allen Spiegel, our editor extraordinaire, and Gretchen Young for their guidance, advocacy, and brilliance.

But most especially to Ethan Hawke, without whom this book would never have existed, or come together so damn well. I love dreaming with you, pard.

—Greg

I just want to thank Greg Ruth.

"You just keep thinking, Butch, that's what you're good at."

—Ethan